# A New Friend

## A lesson on friendship

by Suzanne I. Barchers
illustrated by Mattia Cerato

RED CHAIR ·PRESS·

Please visit our website at **www.redchairpress.com**.
Find a free catalog of all our high-quality products for young readers.

*A New Friend*

Library of Congress Control Number: 2011934550
ISBN: 978-1-937529-04-8 (pbk)
ISBN: 978-1-937529-12-3 (hc)

Lexile is a registered trademark of MetaMetrics, Inc. Used with permission.
Leveling provided by Linda Cornwell of Literacy Connections Consulting.

This edition first published in 2012 by
Red Chair Press, LLC          PO Box 333          South Egremont, MA 01258-0333

Printed in China
1  2  3  4  5  16  15  14  13  12

## A New Friend

The five friends notice their belongings are missing. Have they been robbed? Who would steal their things? Can the friends solve the mystery and find their missing items?

"Hello, Bun," Tab calls. "I brought you some flowers!"
"Come in," says Bun. "I've been up for hours.

I can't find my bracelet. I've looked far and wide.
I hate to give up. But I've tried and I've tried."

"I did find this pin. It has a nice shine.
It is very pretty, but it isn't mine."

"That's strange," Tab says. "My watch is gone, too.
Let's go see Pip. She may know what to do."

"Hi, Pip," says Bun. "We need your help fast.
We are missing some things. This just can not last."

Pip says, "I'm upset too. My new chestnut is gone.
I can't seem to find it. I've been looking since dawn."

They find Sox and Ted. They both look upset.
"We think we've been robbed," Ted says with regret.

Sox says, "We each have things that we just can't find.
The thief, we have noticed, leaves something behind."

"That does it!" says Pip. "I know who's to blame.
It's that packrat, Jack. He thinks it's a game.

12

He swipes things he finds. He goes on house raids.
He'll see something new. Then he just trades."

"It's time to go see him," Tab says, sounding mad.
"It's time that he learns that stealing is bad.

He may be trading and think that's okay.
But sneaking around is not the right way."

"Hi friends," Jack says. "I didn't expect guests.
I'd ask you in, but my den is a mess."

"We're not here as friends," Tab says, "or for fun.
You've taken our things. We know what you've done."

"I'm so very sorry." Jack says with a sigh.
I want to have friends. But I am so shy.

I sneaked in your houses. I took things away.
I'd planned to pretend that I found them one day."

"I thought it would all be okay in the end.
I thought you would like me. I'd be your new friend."

"We'll be your friend, Jack!" Ted says with a grin.
"But we'd like our things back. So let's all begin."

They find their belongings. They clean up Jack's den.

They fill bags with trash, again and again.

The pals work together. They make a new friend.

And Jack gets a nice tidy den in the end.

## Big Questions:

Why are the five friends upset? Why did the packrat Jack take the items from the friends' houses?

Do you think the packrat Jack did the right thing by stealing items? Did the friends forgive Jack for stealing? How do you know?

## Big Words:

**swipes:** takes something quickly

**thief:** someone who steals

**upset:** unhappy, worried

↳ Look at the title of this book. Did you think the story would be about someone who steals things from others? Say how you think Jack felt when the friends helped clean up his house?

↳ Jack thought he would make new friends by pretending to find their things. But stealing is not a good way to make a friend. What are other ways to make a friend?

**Activity**

↳ Make a Friend Frame. Draw a picture of yourself and another person doing something you both enjoy. Decorate the picture with a fun frame and keep it to remind you to forgive.

↳ Are you a packrat like Jack? Do you save everything? Ask a friend or family member to help you put things away so your space is neat and tidy like Jack's den.

## About the Author

**Suzanne I. Barchers**, Ed.D., began a career in writing and publishing after fifteen years as a teacher. She has written over 100 children's books, two college textbooks, and more than 20 reader's theater and teacher resource books. She previously held editorial roles at Weekly Reader and LeapFrog and is on the PBS Kids Media Advisory Board for the next generation of children's programming. Suzanne also plays the flute professionally—and for fun—from her home in Stanford, CA.

## About the Illustrator

**Mattia Cerato** was born in Cuneo, a small town in northern Italy where he still lives and works. As soon as he could hold a pencil he loved sketching things he saw around him. When he is not drawing, Mattia loves traveling around the world, reading good books, and playing and listening to cool music.

 For a free activity page for this story, go to www.redchairpress.com and look for Free Activities.